RUDLEY CABOT IN...

THE QUEST FOR THE
GOLDEN
CARROT

Keith Brumpton

Orion
Children's Books

Contents

A world run by rabbits. And why not?

The author would like to place on record (or CD)
his thanks to all those who helped in the
preparation of this book, especially: Dr Martin
Boot of the Institute of Rabbit Technology for his
advice on spaceships of bygone years; Professor
R. Becker for granting me access to her private
files; and finally to all those on Rabbit Colony
27X for making my stay there such an
enjoyable one.

Keith

6.30 pm, The Odeon 2, Cornwall

First published in Great Britain in 1994
by Orion Children's Books
a division of the Orion Publishing Group Ltd
Orion House
5 Upper St Martin's Lane
London WC2H 9EA

A catalogue record for this book is available from the British Library
Printed in Italy
ISBN 1 85881 045 0 (cased)
ISBN 1 85881 122 8 (paperback)

Episode One

IN A DUSTY BURROW

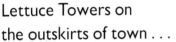

Lettuce Towers on the outskirts of town . . .

Burrow no. 15 . . .

Apartment D . . .

Home of Rudley Cabot . . .

It was a warm, lazy Sunday evening and most of the colony were outside, browsing in the big city. Not Rudley – he was sitting by his computer wishing that something exciting would turn up. He liked turnips.

Suddenly there came an excited THUMP at the burrow door and his sister Cabba rushed in.

Her face was covered
with soil and dust.

Rudley's ears pricked up. This
sounded like adventure.

Cabba led the way as
the two rabbits squeezed
themselves along a whole
system of tunnels they'd
never seen before . . .

With a shove, Rudley forced open the door to the mystery
burrow and shone his torch around the musty-smelling rooms . . .

Episode Two

A MESSAGE FROM THE PAST

WOW, ALL THIS STUFF IS SO UNDER. I'LL BET NO ONE'S BEEN IN HERE SINCE BOB DISAPPEARED...

IS THIS A COMPUTER?

YEAH, IT'S AN OLD CARROTMAC©...

ONE OF THE FIRST RC'S* EVER MADE. THE ONLY OTHER ONE I'VE SEEN IS IN THE HUTCHINSON MUSEUM.

I WONDER IF IT STILL WORKS?

ACCESS FILE

A

E

STAND BY TO RECEIVE MESSAGE

*RC Rabbit Computer: the first computers small enough for a rabbit burrow were invented around R.D. 2038.

RUDLEY TAKES OFF

The next morning Cabba saw Rudley's spaceship parked on the driveway of Lettuce Towers. She felt really worried.

SPACE IS A DANGEROUS PLACE.

IT MUST BE IN THE FAMILY BLOOD.

BYE THEN. AND GOOD LUCK... AND FLY SAFELY!

ZOOOM

Rudley's spaceship was the latest model – the best technology carrots could buy – a CELARI MARK 5.

As the ship took off, Rudley felt a strange **WHOOSH** in his stomach. Mercury-coloured clouds blew past the windscreen. Down below were fields of lettuces and carrots bathed in warm sunshine.

I STOWED AWAY WHILE YOU WERE FILLING UP WITH CAROTIN.* WHAT'S THE MATTER? YOU LOOK PALE.

* **carotin** fuel used in rabbit ships

Rudley was feeling space-sick. It hadn't been like this in *Blade Rabbit* or *Star Paws*.

I DON'T THINK I'VE EVER BEEN THIS HIGH BEFORE. ACCORDING TO THE INSTRUMENTS WE'RE AT 20,000 HOPS...

20,000 HOPS!

HELP!

Space...

...sickness...

...is no fun...

...at all...

A FIND ABOARD THE MOULDY RIND

Captain Weasel was picking his teeth with a piece of old chicken bone…

His ship, The Mouldy Rind, was anchored on the dark side of Rabbit Colony 27X, where Captain Weasel worked as a second-hand spaceship dealer (and a very dodgy one at that).

His crew were a mutinous lot and Captain Weasel treated them badly (unless he wanted something doing).

But when the time was right, his ship would hoist a very different flag – the Jolly Weasel…

Today Captain Weasel was in one of his darkest moods. The used-spaceship lot was filled with rusting wrecks that not even he could hope to sell.

Captain Weasel gave a frustrated growl and went back to his office for a lie down. He switched on his computer to see if he could hack into the in-flight programme of a passing spacefreighter. (This was how he found out which ships carried cargoes that might be worth stealing…)

A cheesy, green-toothed smile spread across Captain Weasel's face. The computer had made a connection…

ACCESS INFORMATION
press 'p'

Weasel drummed his claws on the desk with excitement. The ship he'd made contact with belonged to…

RUDLEY CABOT, EH? A FLUFFY COTTON TAIL SO FAR FROM HOME?

AND WHAT'S THIS MAP? BOB CABOT … THE GOLDEN CARROT…

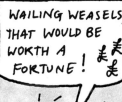

WAILING WEASELS, THAT WOULD BE WORTH A FORTUNE!

WOO-WOO-WOO

The emergency siren woke up the crew of The Mouldy Rind.

HOIST THE JOLLY WEASEL, LADS, LOAD YOUR ELECTRIC CUTLASSES… WE'RE OFF A-PIRATING!

IF WE FIND THE GOLDEN CARROT A FORTUNE WILL BE MINE! ER, OURS…

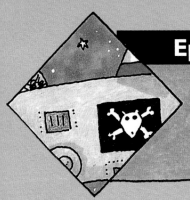

THE JOLLY WEASEL

The Mouldy Rind was an old-fashioned ship, powered by burning rubbish. To get up any speed the crew had to shovel hard. (All except for Captain Weasel, of course!)

← The Captain's hammock

Weasel plotted his course, taking the co-ordinates from Rudley's map.

Suddenly Captain Weasel noticed the presence of another ship on his screen. It was following the same course as his own.

Captain Weasel crept back to his cabin. He had to find a way to make certain that he, and only he, would find the last resting place of The Golden Carrot.

The wayward weasel licked his lips and gave a contented snarl. He'd thought of a plan. A plan that was sure to spell trouble for Rudley and Cabba.

Not far from The Mouldy Rind, Rudley and Cabba had become caught in a space jam.

But too late to stop an intruder boarding his ship...

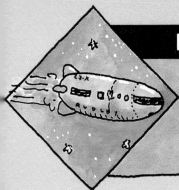

A STRANGER ON BOARD

It had been an exhausting day and Rudley felt relieved when he could finally switch the controls to automatic pilot. Soon both he and Cabba were fast asleep.

Rudley was snoring…

Cabba was dreaming…

Neither of them heard a thing as the mysterious stranger crept towards the engine room…

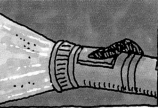

Cabba awoke to the smell of burning rubber. She hopped off to investigate.

But it was too late!

The engine room was on fire!

OH NO!

FIRE! FIRE! RUDLEY, WAKE UP!

Now if there's one thing that rabbits don't like, it's fire. Especially in the engine room!

FIRE EXTINGUISHER

THE FIRE EXTINGUISHER'S GONE! WHAT'S GOING ON HERE?!!

FIRE EXTINGUISHER

It was getting difficult to breathe because of the smoke. Watching from The Mouldy Rind, Captain Weasel gave a squeaky laugh.

His crew shovelled.

And Rudley and Cabba remained trapped aboard their burning ship…

Episode Seven

UP THE SPOUT

Cabba had a plan – a dangerous one. She didn't like danger, but what choice was there? The flames were creeping ever closer…

HIGHLY INFLAMMABLE **DANGER**
NO NIBBLING   NO SMOKING

GOOD LUCK, CAB. I WISH I WAS SMALL ENOUGH TO DO THIS MYSELF…

Cabba lifted the cover of the air vent and peered in. Just room for a small female rabbit. Hopefully…

Ahead of her there was a long, dark tunnel.

It was so narrow she could feel the hot metal against her fur. And she could smell the smoke as it spread through the ship.

Her plan was to reach the water tank at the rear of the ship.

IT'S WORKING!

PHEW!

LOOK, SOMEONE'S OPENED ONE OF THE AIR-LOCKS. AND THE PIPE HAS BEEN CUT... THAT FIRE WAS NO ACCIDENT. IT WAS SABOTAGE!

Just then, Rudley spotted another spaceship close by. He followed her progress on his own radar screen.

Rudley switched on the communication channel.

There was a short delay, then a picture appeared on the screen...

INNOCENT STRANGER OR DEADLY DANGER?

The picture wasn't very clear, probably because there was still a bit of water in the works.

HELLO...

HELLO...

WAS IT YOU WHO CALLED ME?

IT CERTAINLY WAS.

OUR SHIP WAS SABOTAGED LAST NIGHT.

WHAT ARE YOU DOING HERE?

There was a long pause and the inter-ship relay picture went blank for a moment.

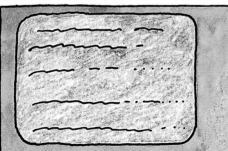

STRANGERS IN THE NIGHT

Midnight arrived, not a paw stirred…

And once again an unexpected visitor arrived without so much as a sound…

Rudley stopped pretending to snore and crept into the corridor. The stranger's shadowy figure was just ahead.

Rudley wondered what to do next. The figure ahead was much too big to tackle alone. He felt a paw on his shoulder.

Without thinking, the two rabbits rushed towards the shadowy saboteur...

It wasn't Rachel Becker after all. It was a tall, ugly-looking weasel... a pirate!!!

The mystery intruder had long teeth and a dark, bristly coat. He seemed surprised to see the two rabbits.

It was then that they remembered…

The world 100 metre record for rabbits was shattered as Rudley and Cabba bobbed at top speed to the control room…

Where they found…
Rachel Becker!

Episode Ten
RACHEL DEFUSES THE SITUATION

worried ← silence

IT'S ALL RIGHT. I'M ONLY INTERESTED IN THE GOLDEN CARROT BECAUSE OF MY RESEARCH.

SHE WAS THE MOST ADVANCED SPACESHIP OF HER DAY. IT WOULD BE WONDERFUL TO LOOK AT HER COMPUTER RECORDS, MAYBE EVEN FIND BOB CABOT'S LOG...

IT WOULD BE SUCH A BREAKTHROUGH IN MY WORK.

Seeing that Rachel only had good intentions, Rudley and Cabba told her the whole story...

LET'S WORK TOGETHER TO FIND THE GOLDEN CARROT.

AND KEEP A LOOK OUT FOR THE MOULDY RIND AT THE SAME TIME.

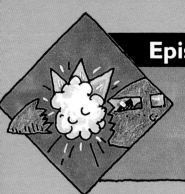

Episode Eleven

ATTACK AT HIGHWAY SEVEN STARS

There were three ships that morning in the sector of Highway Seven Stars...

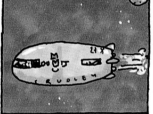

Captain Weasel's....

Rudley and Cabba's...

and Rachel Becker's...

All three were headed for the same spot ...
but where was that spot?

Suddenly Rachel Becker's ship appeared on Captain Weasel's screen.

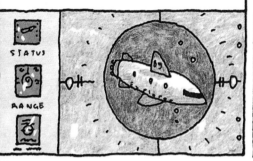

It was a direct hit! Pieces of Rachel's ship disappeared into space and the main hull slowly burnt itself out, lighting up the darkness like a huge firework.

Captain Weasel laughed a pirate's laugh and gave the order to heave-to.

WHAT ABOUT PICKING UP SURVIVORS, CAPTAIN?

THERE ARE NO SURVIVORS.

HA·HA·HA·HA·HA·HA·HA·HO!

But meanwhile, aboard Rudley's ship...

THANKS FOR THE SUGAR.

Rachel had come aboard to borrow some sugar.
THAT SUGAR HAD SAVED HER LIFE!

OH NO! LOOK AT THIS! ER, BAD NEWS, RACHEL, THE MOULDY RIND HAS JUST ATTACKED YOUR SHIP...

IT WAS BLOWN TO PIECES!

ALL MY WORK DESTROYED!

SNIFF.

44

A TRICKY DECISION

Some days later…

Rudley, Cabba and Rachel had followed Bob Cabot's map to the edge of the galaxy, to the exact spot where the record attempt had taken place. But they could find no trace of The Golden Carrot…

IT DOESN'T MAKE SENSE…

HIS SHIP CAN'T JUST HAVE VANISHED.

MAYBE…BUT THE SCREEN IS A COMPLETE BLANK. THERE'S NOTHING OUT THERE…

JUST BLACK.

*__Black hole__ a field of such strong gravitational pull that matter and energy cannot escape from it, presumed to exist where a massive star has collapsed. (In other words, not as nice as a field of lettuces.)

They emerged from the black hole, on the other side of the Galactic Dimension Barrier.
There, before their eyes, lay The Golden Carrot!

Episode Thirteen

SPACE WALK

Rudley didn't like space-walking. (As you probably know, rabbits prefer to hop, but hopping is too dangerous in space.) Even so he couldn't wait to get across to Bob Cabot's ship...

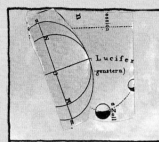

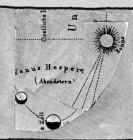

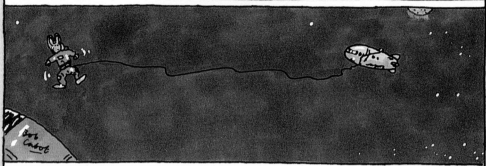

Just as Rudley was about to reach The Golden Carrot, he heard an unmistakable sound: another ship approaching. He recognised the engines at once.

SORRY, FLUFFY COTTON TAIL, BUT THE GOLDEN CARROT IS MINE!

With fiendish accuracy, Captain Weasel cut Rudley's lifeline and the helpless rabbit drifted off into darkest space!!!

Rachel worked out the distances and speed necessary. She knew that any mistake would be fatal. Rabbits don't last long when they're left to drift in deepest space.

The line was fired and sped towards its target. But had Rachel got it right????

Good question!

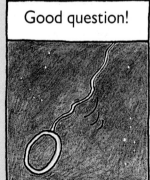

Back once more through the black hole …

Captain Weasel could not believe his eyes. The rabbit ship was on his tail once more!

A HIGH-PACED RACE THROUGH OUTER SPACE

There was chaos aboard The Mouldy Rind. Captain Weasel was in a foul mood. His crew didn't know which way to run.

The strain of trying to tow The Golden Carrot at such high speeds began to take its toll on the pirate ship. She began to creak and groan…

Smoke appeared in the engines…

and finally she spluttered to a halt.

But the engines were broken once and for all.

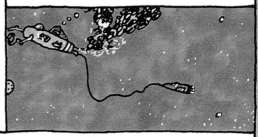

Rudley and Cabba and Rachel were in the observation room when The Mouldy Rind came into view. Rachel guessed at once what had happened.

Nothing happened.

Still no sign of activity...

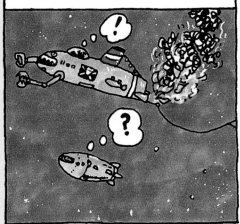

This time, it seemed, he'd gone too far. (About 50,000 miles too far.) The crew of The Mouldy Rind had had enough of Captain Weasel's foul moods and poor cooking. The engine rooms were on fire, the motors were jammed, and enough was enough.

While most of them fled towards the ship's lifecraft, a small party took Captain Weasel prisoner.

BOB CABOT— THE FACTS AT LAST

It was late evening when Rudley finally boarded The Golden Carrot and walked her deserted, ghostly decks.

The ship was really tiny and he had to be careful not to catch his ears on the overhead cables.

HE WAS ONE BRAVE OLD RABBIT TO TRY AND BREAK THE GALACTIC DIMENSION BARRIER IN SOMETHING LIKE THIS.

Rudley switched on his video camera so that Cabba and Rachel could see the inside of the ship as he moved through it.

59

OK. I'M JUST APPROACHING THE FLIGHT DECK NOW. IT'S COMPLETELY DESERTED...

AND I CAN SEE BOB'S SEAT...

JEEPERS!

I'VE FOUND THE CONTROL PANELS. CAN YOU SEE THEM?

THERE'S A SPEED GAUGE... AND IT'S CRACKED... IT'S SHOWING THE SPEED THE GOLDEN CARROT WAS DOING WHEN SHE HIT THE BLACK HOLE...

THAT'S INCREDIBLE!

25,000 HOPS PER MINUTE! YOU KNOW WHAT THIS MEANS DON'T YOU? HE BROKE THE RECORD!

Rudley wiped a tear from his eye. He felt so proud of his ancestor. What must it have been like, all those years ago, as The Golden Carrot accelerated through this lonely edge of the galaxy?

A sudden loss of control…

Sucked into the black hole…

Controls damaged, she travelled faster and faster…

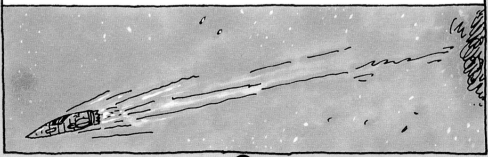

At such a speed, and in so small a ship, Bob Cabot would have been vaporised in a flash...

A sad but glorious end...

Rudley switched off his camera and headed back to the exit hatch. He knew Cabba and Rachel would want to come aboard too...

LETTUCE- GIVE THANKS

The rest of the flight passed smoothly enough. Within a week or so Rabbit Colony 27X came into view. Fields of pale green lettuces shimmered in the early morning sunshine. Carrot tops waved in the spring breeze.

And there was Lettuce Towers..